DISCARD

Information Glut:
Sorting the Good from the Bad

Don Nardo

San Diego, CA

About the Author

In addition to his numerous acclaimed volumes on ancient civilizations, historian Don Nardo has published several studies of modern medical, scientific, and educational topics and phenomena, including *Biomedical Ethics*, *Nanotechnology and Medicine*, *Careers in Education*, *Teen Guide to Mental Health*, *Science and Sustainable Energy*, and award-winning books on astronomy and space exploration. Nardo also composes and arranges orchestral music. He lives with his wife, Christine, in Massachusetts.

© 2023 ReferencePoint Press, Inc.
Printed in the United States

For more information, contact:
ReferencePoint Press, Inc.
PO Box 27779
San Diego, CA 92198
www.ReferencePointPress.com

ALL RIGHTS RESERVED.
No part of this work covered by the copyright hereon may be reproduced or used in any form or by any means—graphic, electronic, or mechanical, including photocopying, recording, taping, web distribution, or information storage retrieval systems—without the written permission of the publisher.

Picture Credits:
Cover: ImageFlow/Shutterstock.com

6: Africa_pink/Shutterstock.com
11: McLittle Stock/Shutterstock.com
14: fizkes/Shutterstock.com
16: GaudiLab/Shutterstock.com
20: supersizer/iStock
23: Anton Garin/Shutterstock.com
24: FG Trade/iStock
31: Ron Adar/Shutterstock.com
34: A katz/Shutterstock.com
36: Ron Adar/Shutterstock.com
40: fizkes/Shutterstock.com
43: GoSlow/Shutterstock.com
45: saeediex/Shutterstock.com
51: Pressmaster/Shutterstock.com
53: SeventyFour/Shutterstock.com
55: Osugi/Shutterstock.com

LIBRARY OF CONGRESS CATALOGING-IN-PUBLICATION DATA

Names: Nardo, Don, author.
Title: Information Glut : Sorting the Good from the Bad / by Don Nardo.
  Description: San Diego : ReferencePoint Press, 2022.
Includes bibliographical references and index.
Identifiers: LCCN 2022012962 | ISBN 9781678203429 (library binding)
  ISBN 9781678203436 (ebook)
Subjects: LCSH: Media literacy--Juvenile literature.

CONTENTS

Introduction   4
Sifting Through the Noise

Chapter One   8
The Causes and Effects of Information Overload

Chapter Two   18
How Information Overload Affects the Brain

Chapter Three   28
Separating Information from Misinformation

Chapter Four   38
The Effects of Information Overload on Teens

Chapter Five   48
Learning to Avoid Information Overload

Source Notes   57
For Further Research   61
Index   63

INTRODUCTION

Sifting Through the Noise

"I have always been addicted to information," states former White House lawyer John Dean. "In college and law school, and until the arrival of the digital era, my idea of a great break was to go to the newsstand to purchase a dozen or more of the latest journals and magazines and do nothing but read them." Later, during the initial years of the digital age, Dean explains, his consumption of information became "far greater, and I [could] lose entire days—even an occasional week—when I [went] on a bender for [I could] multitask and listen in the gym, or when working around the house." Over time, he goes on, he came to rely more and more on digitalized—or computerized—information from his laptop and iPad and became even more of an "information junkie"[1] than before.

"Recently, however," Dean says, "I am not consuming as much information as I did when I used hard copies." For him, the difference is that the more data saturating his digital displays, the less knowledge he retains. "In short, I have been experiencing, for lack of a better term, information anxiety. Or is it information overload? Whatever it is, it['s] the sort of thing that troubles an information junkie."[2]

Drowning in a Sea of Information

As Dean came to learn, the modern term *information overload* refers to the increasingly prevalent situation in which the amount of information people are confronted with is greater than their capacity to effectively absorb it. Put another way, information overload can describe a phenomenon in which a given "system" lacks the capability to process a large volume of data. That system might be a computer or other machine. It also might be the human brain. Whether one is dealing with a computer or a person, each has the capacity to take in, analyze, and remember only so much information. In the case of a human being, if the amount of data exceeds the individual's ability to absorb it, then that person is a victim of information overload.

That term *information overload* was coined in 1964 by the late Hunter College social scientist Bertram Myron Gross. It was subsequently made widely popular by futurist and social commentator Alvin Toffler in his best-selling book *Future Shock*, first published in 1970. Since that time the phenomenon has come to have many other names, such as infobesity, information glut (or "infoglut" for short), information pollution, information anxiety, infoxication, and data fog (or data smog). The late novelist David Foster Wallace called it by still another name: total noise. He compared an individual person's attempt to sift through the noise and make it understandable and manageable to someone drowning without any hope of being rescued.

Examples of the data bits, or individual units of information, that have hugely multiplied over the years can be seen in nearly every area of modern life. There are now millions of printed books and magazines. And online there are billions of internet websites, web articles, emails, tweets, Facebook pages, and other pieces of social media and communication. On top of this are print, internet, and television advertisements as well as numerous TV and cable programs. There are simply far more pieces of data that attract or intrude on people's interest than in past ages.

Adding the uncountable number of salable products to the mix of visual clutter, McGill University psychology professor

Human beings have created vast amounts of data in recent years, leading many people to experience information overload, where they are confronted with more information than they can absorb.

Daniel Levitin writes, "In 1976, there were 9,000 products in the average grocery store, and now it's ballooned to 40,000 products. And yet most of us can get almost all our shopping done in just 150 items. So you're having to ignore tens of thousands of items every time you go shopping."[3] By one calculation, he says, we have created more information in the past ten years than in all of human history before that.

> "In 1976, there were 9,000 products in the average grocery store, and now it's ballooned to 40,000 products."[3]
>
> —Daniel Levitin, McGill University psychology professor

Will Humanity Lose Its Mind?

This incredible accumulation of data is far more than a single human brain is configured to handle. The conscious mind can pay attention to three or maybe four things at once, Levitin points out. "If you get much beyond that, you begin to exercise poorer judgment, you lose track of things and you lose your focus."[4] Memory loss and other serious problems can also occur, problems that could conceivably, some experts warn, make humanity eventually lose its collective mind. Writer and editor Peter Landau briefly sums up the dangers of information overload; the continuing increase in the sheer volume of information confronting society, he says, is ultimately

> "Making a decision takes energy, which is exhausted in the process of gathering data."[5]
>
> —Writer and editor Peter Landau

going to reduce one's ability to make good decisions, making us more prone to logical fallacies. Our minds get tired, and making a decision takes energy, which is exhausted in the process of gathering data. This impacts not only your decision making, but your productivity and ability to stay motivated as well. Does that make you feel anxious? Well, that's another symptom of information overload. . . . We aren't computers, but we can blow our own version of gaskets when we're overloaded with too much data.[5]

CHAPTER ONE

The Causes and Effects of Information Overload

Copywriter and blogger Stephen Altrogge admits to feeling overwhelmed sometimes by the sheer amount of data he must deal with in both his job and personal life. "If you came of age during the 1990's as I did," he says, "then you remember a time before there was widespread internet access. You also remember the sense of amazement you felt at how much information was available to you thanks to these new things called 'search engines.'"[6]

Altrogge calls the pre-1990s period "the good ol' days." It was, he adds, "before we were connected to everyone and everything all the time through our smartphones." It was also "before the advent of emails, tweets, and 24-hour-per-day cable news shows," he says. In those days, he continues, most people did not feel intimidated or overwhelmed by the amount of information that was available to them at any given time. Today, in contrast, he and many other people are gripped by the feeling that "we're all drowning in information," which can be "a truly overwhelming experience."[7]

Moreover, Altrogge cautions that data overload can have negative consequences. He suggests, for instance, that it can have "a significant impact on your productivity and ability to stay focused. When you're constantly bombarded with notifications, texts, chat messages, and emails, you end up in an almost constant state of multitasking. . . . To state the obvious, when you're always in a state of continuous partial attention due to information overload, it's pretty tough to get meaningful work done."[8]

A Mind-Blowing Amount of Information

Recognition of the information overload phenomenon that Altrogge describes is not new. As far back as 1970, Alvin Toffler warned in *Future Shock*, "Today, change is so swift and relentless in the techno-societies [technology sectors] that yesterday's truths suddenly become today's fictions. And the most highly skilled and intelligent members of society admit difficulty in keeping up with the deluge of new knowledge—even in extremely narrow fields."[9]

> "[The most] intelligent members of society admit difficulty in keeping up with the deluge of new knowledge."[9]
>
> —Alvin Toffler, author and futurist

Since Toffler wrote those words, the information revolution he cited has expanded in size many times. In the period from 2020 to 2022, for instance, people worldwide sent an estimated 3 million emails every second of every day. At the same time, more than 500 hours of new content were uploaded to YouTube every minute, and the internet swelled to close to 2 billion websites.

In all, electronic media experts estimate, almost 59 zettabytes of information existed globally in 2020–2022. That is equivalent to 50 billion trillion (or 50 quadrillion) megabytes. Since 1 megabyte equals 1 million bytes (computer talk for individual "pieces" of information), another way to express that mind-blowing total is 50 sextillion bytes (50 followed by 24 zeros). Some scientists translate that amazing figure into astronomical terms, saying that 50 septillion units of information is forty times larger than the number of stars in the observable universe.

As for the causes of this veritable explosion of knowledge, Altrogge mentions the internet and cell phones. But there are literally dozens of others. Hitesh Bhasin, chief executive officer of the online business website Marketing91, summarizes a few others. Nowadays, he begins, news shows of various kinds

> are being produced every single second of the day and made viral so that they can reach more and more people in a short period. The same news is being shared millions of times. . . . Platforms such as television, radio, RSS feeds [online abbreviated overviews of larger articles], mobile phones, emails, social media, etc. are also responsible for causing information overload. . . . [Overall] there [seems to be] infinite information on a single topic.[10]

Confusion, Stress, and an Inability to Filter

Many technology specialists, sociologists, psychologists, and other scientists who have studied the information revolution have expressed worry about the future. They say that information overload's social and personal effects on both individuals and society are more far reaching and detrimental than most people realize. As John B. Horrigan of the well-known polling organization Pew Research Center, points out:

> By the early 2000s, experts were already bemoaning how the volume of digitally driven information could undercut personal productivity, undermine social ties, and foster distraction. The anxious social critic feared that constant flow of digital messages would result in shallow connections among people but not meaningful conversations. It might also create anxiety among people who fear they cannot keep up with information demands.[11]

In addition to making some people feel distracted or anxious, Horrigan and other experts say the information glut can make

A man looks at notifications on his phone. When a person is continually receiving texts, messages, and notifications, it can be difficult to stay focused or be productive.

people feel confused or unsure of themselves. Evidence suggests that reduced decision-making capacity and memory loss can also occur. Furthermore, some people report feeling stressed out because they are so often subjected to so many choices in various areas of their lives.

One major source of such stress, says Indian social commentator Jutimoni Kalita, is that many individuals want to acquire as much useful information as possible, but they regularly underestimate the sheer mass of data they face daily. And the problem becomes how to separate, or filter out, the vital, useful items while ignoring the unimportant, useless ones. She explains:

> People are actually in a hurry to consume every piece of information out there without filtering out the beneficial information among the rest. This can prove to be compromising in terms of the quality of productivity and decision-making ability of the users. The rapid rise of apps and unlimited wireless access has led to oversharing of information and there is no proper mechanism to filter out the important information and dump the rest.[12]

The Expansion of Information over Time

The expansion of human knowledge has been happening for thousands of years. At first it occurred very slowly and moved forward mostly as the result of occasional revolutionary inventions and advances. Two of the biggest were the emergence of writing in the 3000s BCE and the invention of the printing press in the 1400s. In the twentieth century, however, the pace of information expansion accelerated enormously. In the late 1960s scholar Robert Hilliard remarked, "At the rate at which knowledge is growing, by the time the child born today graduates from college, the amount of knowledge in the world will be four times as great. By the time that same child is fifty years old . . . 97 percent of everything known in the world will have been learned since the time he was born." Seed Scientific, an online site that promotes scientific endeavors, keeps track of the many ways that information multiplies and spreads. In 2020, the site states, at least 306 billion emails were sent and received worldwide each day. Also, each day people watched close to 5 billion videos on YouTube, published some 500 million tweets on Twitter, and sent nearly 19 billion text messages.

Quoted in Alvin Toffler, *Future Shock*. New York: Bantam, 1970, pp. 157–58.

Reduced Attention Spans

Still another way, researchers say, that information overload negatively affects individuals and society in general is by shortening people's attention spans. In part this happens because it has gotten easier and easier for people to become distracted from the more basic and important pursuits in life. "We live in a distracted world," remarks Sean Illing, host of the popular Vox *Conversations* podcast, "almost certainly the most distracted world in human history."[13]

One reason for such distraction and subsequent loss of attention span is the excessive amount of time that a majority of people spend online, engaging with social media and other internet sites. In 2020, according to the World Health Organization (WHO), people worldwide spent an average of 145 minutes online each day. That amounts to more than a month per year. Moreover, the WHO made projections about how such online use will continue expanding in the near future. It predicted that a person who begins using the internet at age ten and who lives to be seventy-two will spend a whopping

3,462,390 minutes, or 6 years and 7 months, online. Compare that with an estimated 3 years and 7 months spent eating and drinking and 8 years and 4 months spent watching TV. Indeed, with the huge proliferation of streaming platforms and media outfits in recent years, TV watching—which in decades past had been criticized as a time waster—has become no less of a distraction than online viewing.

In addition, distractions increase and attention spans decrease when people repeatedly check their cell phones for new notifications and jump back and forth among assorted apps to keep from missing something new. With so much happening in society and the world, nearly all of it broadcast online or on TV, people can easily experience what experts call "content fatigue." And so much of this attention grabbing is purposeful. "If you're part of this circus," Illing states, "you're drowning in options and gadgets and screens and you're being pulled in a million directions seemingly all at once. If you spend any time online, you already know this. You're constantly stalked by advertisers and product peddlers, and your attention is constantly being harvested and sold. That's the business model of Big Tech."[14]

British journalist Johann Hari, author of the book *Stolen Focus*, is one of several scholars, journalists, scientists, and others who have described their own diminishing attention spans. He recalls:

> "I noticed that with each year that passed, it felt like my own attention was getting worse."[15]
>
> —Johann Hari, journalist

> I noticed that with each year that passed, it felt like my own attention was getting worse. It felt like things that require a deep focus, like reading a book, or watching long films, were getting more and more like running up and down an escalator. I could do them, but they were getting harder and harder. And I felt like I could see this happening to most of the people I knew. I felt like it was particularly bad for some of the young people in my life, a lot of whom seemed to be worrying at the speed of Snapchat.[15]

Some people say that the existence of so much information makes them feel stressed out because they face so many choices in different areas of their lives.

Initially, Hari says, he dismissed the problem. He assumed it was only natural for someone in his or her sixties and older to have an increasingly short attention span. The older someone gets, he told himself, the more that person's mind deteriorates and the harder it is to keep his or her attention focused on one thing. However, Hari eventually realized that his mind was not growing progressively weaker; rather, he came to realize that the problem was societal in scope and affecting millions of people. The ongoing global glut of information was hindering people's normal ability to focus on items or issues they deemed important. "I came to believe that we really are in a quite serious attention crisis," he told an interviewer, "one that helps us to understand a lot of problems we're facing, both as individuals and collectively. We need to understand that our attention did not collapse. Our attention has been stolen from us by these very big forces. And that requires us to think very differently about our attention problems."[16]

Reduced Workplace Productivity

Hari also makes the crucial point that decreased attention span caused by information overload can negatively affect creating and running a business, as well as being a productive worker in that business. "When attention and focus break down," he writes, "your ability to achieve your goals"[17] in your job significantly diminishes. This echoes Kalita's observation that the global glut of information can compromise productivity.

A clear example of the growing inability of various companies and businesses to absorb and use information can be seen by examining the reams of data that they amass but ignore. According to leading data scientists (experts who measure and analyze large stores of information), most large companies and many smaller ones are quite adept at collecting data. The problem is that they are rarely very good at using that collected information effectively. In fact, an estimated 60 to 95 percent of all the business data collected by global companies is never used to benefit those enterprises.

How Experts Measure Existing Data

When technology experts measure the amount of information that exists at any given moment in time, they usually employ units invented during the digital revolution that began in the second half of the twentieth century. The most basic unit—the byte—generally represents a single, small piece of digitized information. Scientists group bytes into larger and larger units, each 1,000 times larger than the one before it. Hence, a kilobyte is made up of 1,000 bytes, and a megabyte consists of 1,000 kilobytes, or 1 million bytes. In computer-speak, the next step up is a gigabyte, equal to 1,000 megabytes. Then comes a terabyte, equivalent to 1,000 gigabytes, a petabyte, or 1,000 terabytes, and an exabyte, or 1,000 petabytes. After that, the amount of information being measured becomes mind boggling. If one multiplies an exabyte by 1,000, the result is a zettabyte. In 2004, according to technology experts, about 30 exabytes, or 0.03 of a zettabyte, of information existed in the world. A mere ten years later, in 2014, that number had expanded ten times, to 300 exabytes, or 0.3 of a zettabyte. The process is rapidly accelerating because in 2020, just six years later, almost 59,000 exabytes, or 59 zettabytes, of information existed.

> "Gaining control of data should be a key business strategy for any organization."[18]
>
> —The editors of insideBIGDATA, an online technology site

The burning question, of course, is why this occurs. "It seems strange," say the editors of the major technology industry news source insideBIGDATA, "that organizations would let the data lie fallow, especially when that data can make a business more profitable. Gaining control of data should be a key business strategy for any organization." The biggest reason for this colossal oversight, say the insideBIGDATA editors, is that "there is just too much data for them to handle."[18] Even a midsize modern company, they explain, collects or produces many times the total of information handled by any of the largest companies that existed a century ago. Such data collected and produced by companies can consist of the equivalent of hundreds of thousands or even millions of single-spaced typed pages per year.

There is evidence that when people repeatedly check their phones and jump back and forth between various apps to keep from missing anything, their attention spans become shorter over time.

The bottom line is that most companies cannot afford, or in some cases refuse to spend, the money needed to analyze all that information. As a result, the insideBIGDATA editors point out, such businesses

> are missing out on a treasure trove of information they could be using to improve their business models, customer base, and standing in the industry. There's a world of data out there, and each nugget of it can mean more money, more efficiency, and more benefits for organizations. But to realize those benefits, organizations need solutions that . . . [can get] a handle on the huge amounts of data they need to process.[19]

This and other ways that information overload affects businesses are critical to modern society, says Jill Huettich, an expert on digital marketing strategies. This, she says, is "because the global economy has created fierce competition. As a result, it's more important than ever for businesses to develop a smart data strategy and leverage that data effectively." Moreover, considering the several adverse ways that the information glut affects society in general, Huettich says, it is a problem that must not be ignored. "As our society continues to generate more and more information," she cautions, "it looks like the challenges of information overload aren't going away anytime soon."[20]

CHAPTER TWO

How Information Overload Affects the Brain

"I felt like my brain was swelling to the size of a basketball and that it was going to explode at any moment," recalls Iowa educator and writer Lawrence Taylor. "Am I wrong?" he asks. "Or isn't it possible for the human brain to reach some sort of limit at which point it just can't absorb any more information?"[21]

Taylor describes how, besides executing his regular teaching duties, he spent much of his free time researching various topics for articles he writes to publish online. Also, he maintains email correspondences with over fifty former students and feels obliged to read the many articles they send him and comment on those writings in his responses. In addition, he says:

> I try my best to keep up with news and current events. Most evenings I watch one or two evening news programs while grading papers and at the same time answering emails that sometimes come in during those intervals. I have been multitasking like that more and more, and for a while it felt like I was pretty good at it. But over time it got harder and harder and I even started sleeping less so I could take in, analyze, and spit out still more information.[22]

Finally, Taylor recollects, he smacked head-on into what he calls a "wall of reality." By that, he explains, "I mean that I had a major feeling of being overloaded with data, facts, and so forth. The back and forth messages of my bloated correspondence kind of jumbled together and often I couldn't remember who I told what and when I told it. It seemed to me that my brain had simply had enough and had decided to temporarily go on strike."[23]

Learning to Filter What the Brain Vacuums Up

Although Taylor was aiming for humor by describing his brain exploding and going on strike, experts on the brain say that such cartoonish comparisons are not so far from reality. As multiple modern studies of brain functioning attest, the human brain can be overloaded with too much information. Peter Landau points out, "The brain is an amazing tool, . . . but even it has its limits. We often exceed what our brains can process and in so doing reach something called cognitive overload, which means we hit a mental wall that leads to irritability and poor thinking."[24]

Scientists who study the brain use several multisyllable technical terms to describe how the brain works. However, medical researcher and technologist Srini Pillay turns to some simpler terms and ideas that everyone can understand. For example, he likens the brain to "a vacuum cleaner that sucks up information." Such data can consist of visual images, auditory messages that come in through the ears, smells, tastes, and more. "If you leave the brain's vacuum cleaner on its default setting," says Pillay, "it will pick up every piece of information on its path."[25]

> "The brain is an amazing tool, . . . but even it has its limits."[24]
>
> —Peter Landau, writer and editor at ProjectManager

Some of that data, Pillay continues, will be important and worth remembering. But most of the time, much more of it is likely to be trivial and fleeting and not worth remembering. That, he claims, is where information overload can creep in and cause problems. A person often feels compelled to take in and analyze and remember as much information as possible. But the brain lacks the capacity to take it all in. And that can cause confusion, anxiety, and other unwanted responses.

What is needed, therefore, is a kind of brain filter that can sort through the less vital data content and absorb and process the crucial content. "You need to filter information throughout the day,"[26] Pillay states. There are two ways to accomplish this. One is reactive and the other proactive. An example of a reactive filter is when people consciously realize that what they just saw, heard, or read is too much information, or TMI. A sort of self-warning or self-lecture, this reactive filtering sends a message to the brain, telling it not to absorb that piece of information.

In contrast, proactive filtering, according to Pillay, "is a kind of preparation for your brain. Rather than waiting for the TMI moment, you prepare your brain to ignore it. The ding on your Facebook page, for example, is something you can decide ahead of time to ignore, or you could turn notifications off on your computer too."[27]

How Information Is Transformed into Memory

Conscious attempts to keep from becoming overloaded with information like those Pillay describes can be helpful. However,

Many people report that they feel overwhelmed by the constant need to multitask and process large amounts of information.

the modern onslaught of information of all kinds is frequently so powerful and relentless that a lot of unwanted or useless data gets through and becomes memory. Making matters worse, studies of the brain show that once such information is stored in the brain's memory centers, a secondary complication occurs. Namely, many of those memories undergo changes, so that the person has trouble remembering which version of a fact or event is the correct one. With two or more versions each of many memories, there is a sort of multiplying effect. In a sense, the brain is even more overloaded with data than it was before absorbing those bits of information.

Science writers Kaori Ikeda and Hayley Teasdale explain the mechanics of this process, pointing out the reality that the brain does not work the way many people assume. First, they emphasize, the brain does not record things like a camera:

> Many of us think of our memory as being a bit like a recording device—a video camera, say. We imagine it faithfully recording events in detail which we can, at some later stage, retrieve by simply pressing the "play" button.
>
> But this video-camera idea of memory isn't really accurate. That's because memories aren't just static recordings which are "there" to be accessed. Rather, memories are dynamic—they're always changing. They can become stronger or weaker over time. They can become distorted, and they can be manipulated. What we remember and how we remember it depends on when we do the remembering, and what meaning and experience we bring to that memory. In fact, every time we remember something, we alter that memory a little bit.[28]

> "Memories are dynamic—they're always changing. . . . Every time we remember something, we alter that memory a little bit."[28]
>
> —Kaori Ikeda and Hayley Teasdale, science writers

Why Multitasking Is Inefficient and Counterproductive

A 2019 scientific study by Stanford University scholars Kevin P. Madore and Anthony D. Wagner concluded:

> As you go about your day, you may barely notice that you are frequently multitasking. It may be driving to work while listening to a radio program or talking to a loved one on the phone . . . or perusing Facebook while texting a friend, or switching back and forth between a high-level project like compiling a report and a routine chore like scheduling an appointment. Multitasking means trying to perform two or more tasks concurrently, which typically leads to repeatedly switching between tasks (i.e., task switching) or leaving one task unfinished in order to do another.
>
> The scientific study of multitasking over the past few decades has revealed important principles about the operations, and processing limitations, of our minds and brains. One critical finding to emerge is that we inflate our perceived ability to multitask. There is little correlation with our actual ability. In fact, multitasking is almost always a misnomer, as the human mind and brain lack the architecture to perform two or more tasks simultaneously. . . . The human brain has evolved to single task.

Kevin P. Madore and Anthony D. Wagner, "Multicosts of Multitasking," *Cerebrum*, March–April 2019. www.ncbi.nlm.nih.gov.

Further complicating the way incoming information is stored as memories is the fact that there are different types of memories. One is called explicit, or consciously recalled, memory. It consists of events and other data that the person takes specific and clear notice of and feels is important to recall later. Another, more subtle, type of memory is known as implicit, or unconscious, memory, which includes many small details that the average person does not normally consciously pay attention to. Experts point out that other kinds of memory also exist, including procedural memory, by which a person learns basic motor skills.

Still another factor that allows the brain to absorb a lot of information, making it vulnerable to being overloaded, has to do with where the memories are stored. As Ikeda and Teasdale explain:

> Memories aren't stored in just one place in the brain. Rather, different interconnected parts of the brain specialize in different kinds of memories. For example, an area of the brain called the hippocampus [located deep in the brain's lower section] is important for storing memories of particular things that happened in your life, known as episodic memories [information about recent experiences; for instance, what time one awakened this morning or what one ate for dinner last Tuesday].[29]

Meanwhile, remote memories—recollections of events from the distant past—are stored in the brain's neocortex, near the top of the brain; and working memories, involving current information such as the name of someone one just met, are located in the brain's frontal cortex, situated just behind the forehead.

Many people have various social media apps on their phones. Ignoring or turning off notifications for social media sites is one way to stop your brain from becoming overwhelmed with information.

Too Much Information and Elderly Folk

With so many places to store memories, it is perhaps not surprising that the brain can absorb enormous amounts of data. Yet studies of brain function indicate that the more information the brain collects, the less able it is to process all of it efficiently. This is particularly true for people who are older—in their late fifties and beyond.

Hence, the information overload phenomenon worries some members of that age group. In the words of noted New York neurosurgeon Philip E. Stieg, at such an age "we develop what we think are memory problems. We start forgetting where we left our keys, where we parked the car, and wait, who was it that I was supposed to call back? People get frightened, and they make appointments with neurologists because they are afraid they are developing dementia [a serious loss of memory and identity]."[30] In reality, however, most of those people are experiencing information overload rather than dementia.

Researchers have found that older people who worry that they are developing dementia are often simply dealing with information overload.

The exact reasons this happens to many older people is still not completely understood. Some evidence suggests that it has to do with a deteriorating capacity for filtering out less important or useless information. This was the conclusion of an extensive study of the brain published in 2022 by the Rotman Research Institute in Toronto, Canada. Interpreting the study's results, Solarina Ho, a former Reuters news agency researcher, explains:

> As we age, our ability to ignore or filter out irrelevant information weakens, resulting in an overload of information that clutters our memories, according to [the] study. This clutter makes retrieving specific or targeted information, such as when or where an event occurred, more difficult. . . . [This] may explain why our memory becomes more impaired as we age, researchers say.[31]

The Urge to Multitask

All these factors—including the brain's ability to filter data, the existence of multiple memory storage areas, and the increasingly cluttered memories of old age—suggest that the human brain is not "wired" for the modern world's monstrous glut of information. That is the prevailing opinion of neurosurgeons and other experts on the brain's workings. They say that the brain is divided into various areas of function, including language, attention span, visuospatial abilities, memory, and so forth. And that in any given moment or situation, a person must tap into these divided areas one at a time. For this reason it appears that the brain was designed for doing one major task at a time.

Yet the ongoing explosion of data in the information age has encouraged many people to try to force their brain to do multiple tasks at the same time—so-called multitasking. Moreover, it is not uncommon for people to view the ability to multitask as evidence of their intellectual prowess or superiority. But as Stieg warns, it is questionable whether multitasking is an actual ability in the first place. In fact, he points out, the attempt to multitask is rarely, if ever, as effective as people expect or hope it will be. "Your brain works best," he explains,

> when it does one thing at a time, with all your attention focused on the task at hand, without disruption. Can you even remember the last time you accomplished anything that way? We have become accustomed to multitasking, and we fool ourselves into thinking that it makes us more efficient. But if we answer an email while we're talking on the phone as we're walking the dog . . . we're not doing any of those things well, and we're working against evolution as well.[32]

Lessening Information Overload's Assault on the Brain

Based on recent research, medical technologist Srini Pillay recommends regular exercise as an effective way to combat the negative effects of information overload on the brain.

> Your brain consumes 20% of the body's energy even though it only uses 2% of the body's volume. This means that when your body lacks energy, your brain will suffer too. This is probably why conditioning your body with yoga can improve your quality of life, or why exercise helps your body manage its energy more effectively. Doing either also gives your brain a break. Building time in your day to take your mind off your work will help to rejuvenate your brain. When you organize your day with these principles in mind, you will have a new, improved day *sculpted* to manage information overload. . . . When things start getting overwhelming, go for a walk to make connections or use local feedback control [i.e., reflecting on the here and now]. Practice using these techniques often, and you will likely increase your brain's efficiency significantly, and you may improve your quality time at home as well.

Srini Pillay, "The Ways Your Brain Manages Overload, and How to Improve Them," *Harvard Business Review*, June 7, 2017. https://hbr.org.

Stieg's negative view of multitasking is based on studies that show that, like the bigger problem of information overload that encourages it, frequent multitasking can make a person feel stressed out. Confusion, anxiousness, and exasperation are other typical outcomes of regular multitasking. Much of the problem, the experts say, stems from the brain's finite, or limited, speed of processing and filtering incoming information. By trying to multitask, they point out, a person demands that his or her brain process and filter faster than it is designed to do.

> "We have become accustomed to multitasking, and we fool ourselves into thinking that it makes us more efficient."[32]
>
> —Philip E. Stieg, neurosurgeon

This does not mean that people should shy away from trying to learn new things as quickly and efficiently as possible, writes internet content marketer Jory MacKay. After all, he says, "that constant search for new, better, or novel information can empower as much as overwhelm us. Unfortunately, the line between the two is razor thin. . . . The answer isn't to be less informed. It's learning how to search out, consume, and filter it in the best way possible."[33]

CHAPTER THREE

Separating Information from Misinformation

The COVID-19 pandemic that began in late 2019 and continued on its destructive path into 2022 is a tragedy of epic proportions. By March 2022 the United States had more than 79 million documented cases of COVID-19. Nearly 1 million of those cases were fatal. Worldwide, the figures were 448 million cases of the disease, just over 6 million of which ended in death.

The sheer scope of the pandemic—characterized by months of uncertainty, fear, sickness, and death—created a sort of perfect storm for the growth of information overload and the spread of misinformation. Despite abundant evidence of the pandemic's effects, large numbers of people believe the crisis has been exaggerated. Some have even argued that COVID-19 is not real—that it is a manufactured crisis designed to spread fear and take away people's freedoms.

Too Much Information

Views like these result from a variety of factors. One is the enormous amount of information—some reliable and verifiable and some without any basis in fact—found online, on television, and in other forms of media. The sheer mass of stories and information related to the pandemic has made it difficult for people to separate fact from fiction, or real news from fake news. "Unable to process all this material," college science professors Filippo Menczer and Thomas Hills explain, "we let our cognitive biases decide what we should pay attention to. These mental shortcuts influence which information we search for, comprehend, remember, and repeat to a harmful extent."[34]

To illustrate this idea, Menczer and Hills describe a scenario involving a man they call Andy. Andy was working at a hotel when the epidemic first surfaced in the United States. There were many stories about COVID-19 in various news outlets, including on the radio, television, and internet. Andy did not have time to read and absorb them all. So he came to rely on snippets of information shared by friends on social media.

As time went on, Andy began to wonder whether the pandemic might be exaggerated. One of his friends posted an article online that suggested that COVID might be a scary story made up by large drug companies working alongside corrupt politicians. And because he already felt distrustful of government, this seemed to make sense to him. He went online and found some sites that claimed that the virus was no worse than flu. In fact, Andy did not personally know anyone who had died of the disease. Eventually, all these factors came together to make him conclude that COVID-19 was probably just a hoax.

Unreliable Sources

It did not occur to Andy that the sources of the information he was seeing might not be knowledgeable or reliable. This problem has become increasingly common, notes Hitesh Bhasin, as

> high-quality phone cameras and the accessibility to high-speed internet have made every third person on the street a news reporter. This not only created information overload but also created an abundance of inaccurate and

baseless information and the same information is copied and shared over and over again in a different form without checking the validity of the platform.³⁵

The key to understanding how the scenario Bhasin describes occurs is not to blame the technical devices themselves. Rather, it is how they are handled, or more accurately mishandled, that can cause problems. When no major barriers exist to acquiring large amounts of information, University of Michigan psychology professor David Dunning points out, the door is opened to increasingly larger numbers of people providing it. And a hefty proportion of them deal more in opinion than fact.

> "High-quality phone cameras and the accessibility to high-speed internet have made every third person on the street a news reporter."³⁵
>
> —Hitesh Bhasin, chief executive officer of the online business website Marketing91

Before the rise of the internet, Dunning and other experts say, most public information came from published books and magazine articles and radio and TV news programs. These were largely vetted by experts. And most people who advanced misinformation, either out of ignorance or on purpose, were relegated to fringe publications that were easily identified as such.

All that changed as the internet exploded in the 1990s, rapidly expanding the ongoing information age. Regrettably, Dunning says, among the much larger numbers of information providers, most are misinformed or "bad actors" with various reasons to distort the truth. "Thus, when all is said and done," he states, "we now have the technology to send information around the world in a nanosecond but have no way to ensure that this information is worth paying attention to."³⁶ And since the internet does not establish a hierarchy of websites, online sources may appear to be of equal value and standing in the information marketplace.

> "We now have the technology to send information around the world in a nanosecond."³⁶
>
> —David Dunning, University of Michigan psychology professor

A protester is pictured at an anti-mask and anti-vaccine mandate rally in 2021 in New York City. Many online sites contain misinformation about COVID-19 and have convinced large numbers of people that the pandemic is not real or has been exaggerated.

As for the worthless information to which Dunning refers, which stems in large part from the vast data fog that has come to envelop society, there are two main types. One, misinformation, is usually defined as wrong or distorted facts caused by ignorance or honest error on the part of the person who conveys it. Often, misinformation is spread by well-meaning people who think they are providing legitimate facts. The other type of worthless data is disinformation, or wrong facts purposely propagated by people who know full well they are doing harm. Meanwhile, Dunning points out, the truth is out there, although "it is increasingly hidden behind curtains of deception, misdirection, and misinformation."[37]

Feedback Loops and Bad Actors

Whether information overload stimulates and supports misinformation or disinformation, the ultimate effect is frequently the same. Namely, wrongheaded data is continually reproduced and quoted in a constantly multiplying spiral of online articles, Facebook posts,

Potentially Deadly Disinformation About the Pandemic

Of the numerous pieces of disinformation about the COVID-19 pandemic that were driven by information overload, says the Alliance for Science's Mark Lynas, is the false charge that doctors and the government have majorly exaggerated the disease's death rates. According to this assertion, wearing masks and social distancing measures were never needed. "Prominent in promoting this myth," Lynas says,

> is Dr. Annie Bukacek, whose speech warning that COVID death certificates [were] manipulated has been viewed more than a quarter of a million times on YouTube. Bukacek appears in a white lab coat and with a stethoscope around her neck, making her look like an authoritative medical source. Dig a little deeper, however, as *Rolling Stone* magazine did, and it turns out she's actually a far-right anti-vaccination and anti-abortion activist, previously noted for bringing tiny plastic fetuses into the Montana state legislature. Her insistence that COVID death rates [were] inflated has, of course, no basis in fact. More likely the [disease's] death toll is a serious under-count."
>
> To further clarify the issue, the Centers for Disease Control and Prevention has published information on its website about excess deaths associated with COVID-19.

Mark Lynas, "COVID: Top 10 Current Conspiracy Theories," Alliance for Science, April 20, 2020. https://allianceforscience.cornell.edu.

tweets, and other digital venues. A fair amount of that misguided information is then quoted and further perpetuated by radio and television reports, speeches by politicians, and other means. In this way, the endless repetition of poor information initially driven by information overload causes that overload to become even bigger. This is called an information feedback loop. Clearly, the more the accumulated information feeds back on itself, the larger the data glut becomes.

Such a feedback loop can grow on its own as the result of simple misinformation. But more often it develops by the intervention of a person or persons who purposely want to cause mischief or damage. During the 2016 US presidential campaign, for example, Russian hackers planted thousands of online articles, Facebook pages, tweets, and so forth that spread false rumors about Democratic candidate Hillary Clinton. These rumors then multiplied through feedback loops, with the result that millions of Americans were regularly exposed to fake information about her. There was so much of it, so often, that some voters assumed there must be something to it. Many political experts say that this was one of the key factors in Clinton's loss of the race to Republican Donald Trump.

This same insidious problem has been poisoning political and other discourse in the country ever since. Those individuals trying to blur the line between fact and fiction through information overload include not only Russian, North Korean, and other malicious foreign governments but also operatives of US political parties, various interest groups, and scattered individuals with extremist views. According to Mike Loukides, an editor for O'Reilly Media:

> "For the last few years, we've been trapped in a nightmare of feedback loops."[38]
>
> —Mike Loukides, editor for O'Reilly Media

> For the last few years, we've been trapped in a nightmare of feedback loops, where abuse and fake news feed on more abuse and fake news to produce noise. The noise can be targeted precisely at people, at issues, and at organizations. It quickly makes rational discussion impossible; that's its point. This process has been weaponized by bad actors, both domestic and international, ranging from teenagers in Macedonia to informally organized networks of [American] "patriots" . . . to professional groups like Russia's Internet Research Agency, that can mount very sophisticated attacks. The content of the howl isn't even important, except to the extent that it destroys the possibility for normal conversation.[38]

Information Overload and Conspiracy Theories

In addition to creating confusion, spreading false rumors, and hindering normal conversation, information overload both spawns and strengthens attempts to make fictional ideas and narratives appear to be factual. This is the basis of what have long been described as conspiracy theories. Such a theory, which usually takes the form of a nasty accusation, is that sinister groups of people—often in positions of authority—are secretly working together in a coordinated manner. Their goal, supposedly, is to commit crimes or various dastardly acts that are harmful to society.

Not only are conspiracy theories typically untrue, they also frequently contain major elements that make no sense at all or are even downright ridiculous when examined closely and soberly. Typical is the absurd claim that the National Aeronautics and Space Administration oversees a prostitution ring on Mars. Also, during the 2016 campaign, Clinton supposedly abused children in satanic rituals in the basement of a Washington, DC, pizza parlor.

Hillary Clinton speaks at a rally in New York City in in 2016. During the 2016 presidential campaign, hackers planted thousands of online posts with false rumors about Clinton. The information was repeated so often that many voters thought it was true.

Conspiracy Theories Enhanced by the Information Glut

According to University of Kent social psychologist Karen Douglas, a conspiracy theory is "a proposed plot carried out in secret, usually by a powerful group of people who have some kind of sinister goal." Although conspiracy theories have existed for centuries, she explains, they have become especially prevalent in recent decades. This, several experts suggest, is partly because of the enormous amount of information distributed online. It is not unusual, for instance, for there to be hundreds, thousands, or even tens of thousands of online articles about a single topic or subtopic. In response, people follow certain trends when trying to cope with this veritable avalanche of information. One trend, experts say, is when viewers look only at a small number of sites related to a specific topic because it would be too time consuming and daunting to look at all the sites about that topic. Moreover, the few sites they do look at tend to be solely those that support the conspiracy. Thus, Douglas says, the evidence for such a theory "is really quite limited and only drawn from a particular type of sources," which partly explains how someone might come to accept a highly outlandish idea.

Quoted in American Psychological Association, "Speaking of Psychology: Why People Believe in Conspiracy Theories, with Karen Douglas, PhD," 2021. www.apa.org.

In a similar vein, several examples of such false accusations developed during the COVID-19 pandemic that swept the world during 2020 to 2022. As Dr. Jessica Justman, an infectious disease expert at Columbia University, explains, the flood of daily news stories and statistics generated during the pandemic greatly expanded global information overload. In turn, she says, that made it harder than ever for many people to separate fact from fiction and rumor from deliberate efforts to mislead. Amid the outbreak, she said that "there's so much information out there that many people are just saying 'I can't read it, it makes me too anxious.'"[39]

It is not surprising, therefore, that this deluge of data created fertile ground for rumor mills to generate conspiracy theories about COVID-19. Only a few of the many absurd, easily disproved stories that spread during that period were that 5G transmission towers spread the coronavirus; that eating bananas prevents people from catching the disease; that the vaccines developed to fight COVID-19 contain microchips implanted by billionaire Bill Gates so that he can rule the world; that the tireless medical expert and humanitarian Dr. Anthony Fauci personally manufactured the virus to use as a biological weapon so that he, too, could rule the world; and that COVID-19 does not actually exist but is instead part of a nefarious scheme by a gang of evil rich people trying to take away people's freedoms.

Such preposterous ideas are driven not only by information overload but also by what psychologists and other experts call

People who believe the COVID-19 vaccine is really just a way to microchip the general public talk at a rally in New York City in 2021. A deluge of online data about COVID-19 has led to the creation and spread of many conspiracy theories.

confirmation bias. Those guilty of it most often seek out only the information that confirms what they already believe. Moreover, they look for data that seems to confirm that they and other members of their group are important or good or worthy. That group might be a specific political party, religion, profession, or some other category. The confirmation of that group's goodness or importance, of course, comes at the expense of "outsiders," who are typically viewed as somehow bad or unworthy. As University of Kent social psychologist Karen Douglas explains it, most conspiracy theory believers are

> people who have an overinflated sense of the importance of the groups that they belong to, but at the same time, the feeling that those groups are underappreciated. [Such] feelings [tend to] draw people towards conspiracy theories, especially conspiracy theories about their groups. So in having those sorts of beliefs, you can maintain the idea that your group is good and moral and upstanding, whereas others are the evil doers out there who are trying to ruin it for everybody else.[40]

Reversing the Trend?

In these ways, information overload works in tandem with already existing and quite natural human frailties to confuse, mislead, fool, or upset people of all walks of life. Misinformation and disinformation have regrettably become deeply imbedded within the social fabric. To reverse that trend will likely be a difficult goal to achieve, say Menczer and Hills, yet one that must be pursued by citizens who care about the country and the truth. "To restore the health of our information ecosystem," they write, "we must understand the vulnerabilities of our overwhelmed minds and how the economics of information can be leveraged [used] to protect us from being misled."[41]

CHAPTER FOUR

The Effects of Information Overload on Teens

In 2021 Kevin Diaz, then a student at the University of North Texas, wrote an article for the school newspaper. "The brutal but obvious truth," he stated in print, is that "we are hopelessly caught in a state of overstimulation."[42] This was his colorful way of denoting the immense fog of data often called information overload.

Like many other modern students in their teens and early twenties, Diaz could not help but feel the weight of that overabundance of information constantly pressing on him. He was aware that neither he nor any of his fellow students were intellectually capable of absorbing and analyzing even a small portion of that daily blizzard of data. There could be no doubt, he remarked in the article, that "more information is being generated right now that would take millions of lifetimes to digest. Being in the know in current events, entertainment, pop culture, or really anything is a futile effort. Today's definition of staying current focuses more on how much information your brain can retain instead of what is *being* retained."[43]

Not only does the information glut feel overwhelming to teens and other students, Diaz wrote, it also negatively affects the way they view and deal with facts about the world around them. In his words:

The overflowing of information causes us to be more callous and numb to emotional events. There is bound to be emotional disconnection when one encounters national tragedies and proceeds to scroll down to the next shiny object instead. It also does not help when news of moral crises depress viewers rather than encourage social change. . . . Our mental and emotional well-beings veer to what we see on our phones, which itself is shaped by our preferences. It is a cycle of unsatisfaction, dense with material that ultimately does little for our betterment.[44]

A Plethora of Sources and Devices

Diaz suggested that students' cell phones are conduits to a seemingly dense undergrowth of information entangling society in innumerable ways. That vast thicket of data is generated by many sources, all of which target young people with an unusual degree of intensity. In part, this is because teens and other students tend to be highly adept at using the latest digital devices.

Some of the sources students use for information are the same ones that adults, businesses, and various organizations use. These include online websites and podcasts; Facebook, Twitter, Instagram, Snapchat, TikTok, and other similar social media; television and radio programs and commercials; and to a lesser degree, newspapers, magazines, journals, and books. However, in regard to the digital world, young people are alert to trends, popular sites, memes, and other facets of those information systems in ways that older users are not. They were born into that world and can navigate it with ease, even if that does not make them immune to that form of information overload.

> "Our mental and emotional well-beings veer to what we see on our phones."[44]
>
> —Kevin Diaz, University of North Texas student

In addition, students in their teens and early twenties are targeted by information sources because of their age. For example,

An overabundance of information leads some teens to feel emotionally disconnected from serious national events; they read about something, then quickly scroll to the next thing that catches their attention.

young people are classified as students and therefore receive a variety of input from what are collectively called "school information sources." According to SchoolCNXT, an organization that strengthens relationships among local schools, students, and students' parents, "Families are getting bombarded by school information from so many sources that they don't know what to pay attention to." In a typical school district, for instance, "information goes through emails, robocalls, phone calls, social media accounts, the district website, and live-streamed meetings, to name only a few."[45]

Moving from the district level down to that of an individual school brings a different set of information sources into play, SchoolCNXT points out. Frequently, individual schools have their own websites, separate from the district's site. Also, schools contact parents and students using their own telephones, email systems, letters and forms from the school administration, and so forth. In a like manner, individual teachers sometimes have their own websites, personal lists of rules and newsletters, and the like. Meanwhile, both individual parents and parents working together in committees send emails, letters, texts, social media posts, and other forms of communication to teachers, administrators, and students.

This is just one way the information marketplace groups and targets young people. Athletic organizations, product advertisers, fashion retailers, and social media sites are only a few of the other information sources that use sophisticated and varied means of reaching students and other youth categories.

Perpetuating Feelings of Hopelessness and Helplessness

The overall result of having so many dozens of separate sources disseminating data to students within a given month, week, or day is a classic example of information overload. "Messages get lost when there are too many sources," SchoolCNXT points out. "Information is flowing from so many spigots that it's impossible to filter out what is critical or even relevant."[46] This can leave teens and other students feeling confused, bewildered, disoriented, or uncomfortable.

However, the adjective most often used to describe students' reactions to information overload is *overwhelmed*. In 2020 Rachel Neha Shaw, a student in the Duke University Center for Global Women's Health Technologies, asked groups of students in their late teens how they felt most often after reading the news or watching news programs for an hour or more. Some 82 percent of them responded that they felt at least somewhat overwhelmed, and over 65 percent reported feeling extremely overwhelmed.

Typical was the reaction of one of the students Shaw approached, who pointed out that as the number of news sources increased, the more the overall accuracy of the news reported was in question. "Access to technology has made me receive almost more information than I'd like," that student said. "I love that it helps me stay informed because I wouldn't be nearly as informed without technology, but sometimes there is too much fake news and rumors."[47]

A Student Wants Just Enough News to Feel Aware of Global Events

In 2020 Rachel Neha Shaw of the Duke University Center for Global Women's Health Technologies conducted numerous interviews with North Carolina students in their late teens. The main topic was information overload and its effects on students. Typical of the replies was this one:

> I do not regularly check the news on my own, and I don't make an effort to be aware of political or social events (which is not something I'm proud of). So for me it's kind of nice to just have those things brought to my attention on occasion so that I'm aware of what's going on in the world. When I am just scrolling through social media, even on Instagram, videos about the government or environmental protests will pop up and it can be, as I've said, nice to have current events brought to my attention. But once you click on one of those, if you keep scrolling, more and more similar posts come up and it can get overwhelming to the point that I don't feel like I'm learning anything and I just have to turn it off and take a breather.

Quoted in Rachel Neha Shaw, "Information Overload: How Much Is Too Much?," Mustang Monthly, April 10, 2020. https://khsmustangmonthly.com.

Another of the students who answered Shaw's questions addressed the issue that information overload makes many young people feel useless and hopeless. The impression that student received from watching the news was that the world is a vast quagmire of problems and troubles that no single person could ever do anything to remedy. The data glut in news and other information, the student stated, has "made us desensitized to issues that would've been taken much more seriously previously, like school shootings or global conflict. It has also made us as a generation seem a tiny bit hopeless in that these issues are so far away and we can only do so much to help."[48]

Teachers' Impressions of Their Students

On the far larger scale of national education, the well-known polling organization Pew Research Center has found similar expressions that young people feel overwhelmed by the amount of information they are exposed to. However, Pew found, the proportion of students who feel that way has changed somewhat over time. Back in 2006 Pew interviewed more than one thousand young people and found that almost 30 percent of them felt very overwhelmed by the growing data glut. It is revealing that a decade later, in 2016, Pew found that only 20 percent of the students interviewed felt dazed or burdened by information overload. That suggests that over time some young people may be growing increasingly accustomed to dealing with large amounts of information.

However, the Pew researchers suspected that those figures might be skewed somewhat by the personal biases of the interviewees. That is, some or even many of the young people polled might have felt more overwhelmed by the data glut than they were willing to admit. What made the researchers think this were the results of a 2013 Pew study of thousands of teachers, who were asked how adept their students seemed to be at handling large masses of data. An alarmingly high figure of 83 percent of

A girl takes a break from looking at her laptop. Researchers have found that a significant percentage of students feel overwhelmed when they read about news or watch news programs.

the teachers had responded that their students were often overwhelmed by information overload.

Almost all the teachers interviewed had also agreed that the internet and other digital technology tools are crucial sources of information for modern students. Yet those same tools can promote distracted behaviors when students use them for entertainment or to communicate with friends on social media. A whopping 87 percent of the teachers polled agreed with the statement "Today's digital technologies are creating an easily distracted generation with short attention spans."[49]

> "Students' default position is [often] to believe whatever search engines give them in their query responses."[50]
>
> —Lee Rainie, Pew Research Center researcher

Moreover, many of the teachers in the poll made the point that in addition to becoming distracted, many of their students have demonstrated a diminishing ability to think critically. According to this view, the sheer number and variety of information sources are so large that many students are unable to separate trustworthy sources from untrustworthy ones. One of Pew's leading researchers, Lee Rainie, says the teacher poll indicated that "students aren't necessarily equipped to know if the information is coming from reliable and respected sources. [The teachers] worry that their students' default position is to believe whatever search engines give them in their query responses."[50]

Some Disturbing Trends

If the tendency of many students to find and use unreliable information seems disturbing, it is one of the least worrisome aspects and outcomes of information overload. Experts have identified some other less-than-desirable trends. One is that large numbers of students in their teens and early twenties have developed a distorted sense of the passage of time. This happens because new information is constantly replacing and overshadowing older information. As Shaw points out, "With information constantly being released and available, new issues and happenings often

The 2020 funeral of Qassem Suleimani in Iran is shown. Suleimani was assassinated in a US drone strike, yet news of his death was quickly forgotten as young people became distracted by other stories.

crowd our own concept of time and certain events' relativity to today in terms of how 'far away' or long ago they feel to people."[51]

To demonstrate this troubling phenomenon, Shaw worked the killing of Iranian military officer Qasem Soleimani by a US drone on January 3, 2020, into her interviews with students. In the days that followed that event, she says, it remained in the forefront of global news broadcasts. Yet it did not take long for most teenagers and other students to put Soleimani's demise in the rearview mirror, so to speak. By early February the onrush of fresh news stories caused most young people to forget about the killing. Then, in March, Shaw later recalled,

> I asked the respondents to my survey how far away the events of January 2020 felt to [them] . . . and 81.1% of students responded that the events felt like they occurred

very long ago and much further away than they recalled or expected. This perceived distance from the present demonstrates how information overload can clog, in a sense, the passage of time and how far away certain events feel to people, regardless of how close to the present they may have occurred.[52]

Another disturbing trend that information overload has helped bring about is a markedly decreased use of traditional, reliable information sources by students. These include printed books and journals, as well as librarians, scientists, and other bona fide experts. Correspondingly, there has been an increased reliance by students on digital devices and internet sites that sometimes produce less dependable data. "While it is not surprising to find

Setting Limits on Student Technology Use

Although the negative effects of information overload on teens and other students remain widespread and well imbedded in society, some educators and education support groups have suggested ways to alleviate them. SchoolCNXT, an organization that builds relationships among local schools, teachers, and students, for example, suggests that parents and teachers set some basic limits on students' use of technology. "Parents can keep phones out of students' bedrooms at night," the group states, "limit data plans, or could turn off wireless internet in the house in the evening. These are small steps, but any time that a student isn't 'plugged in' is a time when the messages they receive are limited and more controlled." Also, SchoolCNXT proposes, schools can monitor student use of digital devices. "This is one reason for providing school-owned devices for students—they can be monitored as opposed to a 'bring your own device' model, where monitoring is much harder." In addition, SchoolCNXT advises parents and teachers to ask students questions about what they see and learn online. Hopefully this can keep lines of communication open and provide support for the students if unforeseen problems arise.

SchoolCNXT, "Information Overload from Too Many School Communications Sources," July 10, 2021. www.schoolcnxt.com.

that students rely on the internet and various online tools and platforms to conduct research," Rainie writes, "the degree to which these resources dominate their research is noteworthy."[53] Pew found that 94 percent of students regularly use Google or other online search engines to do research. Also, 75 percent use Wikipedia or other online encyclopedias, and 52 percent use YouTube or social media sites. Only 12 percent of students, Pew found, primarily get their information from traditional printed books.

> "Information overload can clog, in a sense, the passage of time."[52]
>
> —Rachel Neha Shaw, Duke University student

Some educators talk about trying to reverse these and other similar trends. But little headway has yet been made in such efforts. For the present, says Kelly Bielefeld, who teaches at Friends University in Wichita, Kansas, people must be content to acknowledge the problems information overload creates and to discuss ways to deal with them. "It is a changing world," he says, "and our students are in uncharted territory when it comes to these issues. If parents, teachers, and schools can work together, they can create a safer environment for students to grow up in and limit the different messages they receive about life."[54]

CHAPTER FIVE

Learning to Avoid Information Overload

"Up until recently, I stuffed my brain with information like a hung-over heavyweight [boxer] fills his belly at a Las Vegas all-you-can-eat buffet," says Chris, a popular Canadian blogger. Typically, he recalls, he listened to multiple podcasts while "skimming through email newsletters, while eating." Why not multitask like that? he repeatedly asked himself. "Knowledge is power, right? I figured that one day being so 'well-informed' would come in handy. And I thought it made me smarter."[55]

The problem, Chris continues, was that over time his brain became overwhelmed, and he increasingly had days when he felt "on edge, jittery, and restless. My right eyelid even started twitching." He jokes that "it was as if I had developed Type II information diabetes. I was consuming way more information than I needed. My brain's inability to process it all made me crave more and more. And it was making me unwell."[56]

Then something happened that turned Chris's life around, and for the better. His wife had a baby, and like most new parents, the couple got caught up in the time-consuming duties of taking care of a newborn. Suddenly, Chris no longer had the time to consume large amounts data in the way he had before. At first, he assumed that was a bad thing, but steadily he came to suspect that it might be just the opposite. To help him figure out which of those assumptions was true, he remembers, "I decided to try an experiment. For over a month, I avoided trying to absorb any information other than how to change diapers."[57] Then, at a very slow pace, he began absorbing information again through reading, listening to podcasts, and so forth.

It did not take long for Chris to realize that something fundamental within him had changed. In a nutshell, he recollects, "my palate was pickier." He realized that much, if not most, of the data spewed out by his usual sources was no longer appetizing or compelling to him. Clearly, he concluded, devouring what he now saw as "trivial trivia" had long prevented him from doing and enjoying "cool *real* things" in his life. "So I dramatically shifted and slimmed down my information diet toward only consuming what could make a marked difference in my real life,"[58] he says.

Chris became especially wary of looking at information that would feed his confirmation bias. "You're not helping anyone if you only consume information that confirms what you already know so that you can keep doing what you're already doing. On the contrary, you are cementing your status as a hardheaded, self-justifying echo-chamber-dweller."[59] That realization motivated him to spend more time considering other people's opinions on important issues.

> "You're not helping anyone if you only consume information that confirms what you already know so that you can keep doing what you're already doing."[59]
>
> —Chris, Canadian blogger

Needed vs. Unneeded Information

The main lesson Chris learned—a recognition that changed his life in positive ways—was not that information is bad or damaging or something to be avoided. Rather, he came to realize that some of the data that bombards the average person in the ongoing information age is necessary, helpful, and healthy. But much of that incoming stream of information is unnecessary, burdensome, and in certain instances unhealthy. And most importantly, people can learn how to absorb the healthy portions of that stream while filtering out the unhealthy portions. Author, Peter Landau ably sums up this general approach to countering information overload, saying:

> We live in an information-saturated age and at times it might feel impossible to avoid. Most don't have the luxury to go off the grid or join a monastery. But that doesn't mean one should throw up their hands, give up, and jump in the endless stream of data to drown in bits and bytes. The Buddhists speak of a middle path, which is just moderation. It's a sober way to approach information, where sobriety means restraint rather than abstinence. The idea that one can avoid information is ridiculous and not practical. But there are ways to not overindulge.[60]

Several technology, media, and marketing experts, educational groups and websites, and others recommend strategies to combat the tendency to overindulge. Nearly all agree that the first step is to prioritize the incoming data; that is, people should decide what information is important and useful to them and what is extraneous. Alternatively, people might prioritize by determining what information needs to be dealt with right away and what can wait until a later time to address.

Perhaps the simplest way to go about that separation of needed data from unneeded data, most experts say, is to make lists of one's personal activities, along with the traditional information sources one uses. "Have you made the lists?" ask the editors of IvyPanda, a popular online site that connects students to academic experts. Once the list of daily or weekly tasks is made, an individual can set priorities and evaluate the relative importance of those duties. According to IvyPanda's editors, this allows a person to "decide in what order to complete them. You will see that some can wait for another day, week, or even month. So, wisely plan your time and workload, and you won't feel overwhelmed."[61]

It is common for people to multitask in order to absorb multiple types of information at once. However, this can cause the brain to become overwhelmed.

Meanwhile, IvyPanda's editors recommend, ignore any data that seems completely unneeded, along with the sources of that information. "Have you identified your key information websites that correspond to your interests? Focus on them and eliminate the other sources. You won't get any critical insights from there, so why would you fill your head with unnecessary news?"[62]

Another way of prioritizing, marketing expert Renee Goyeneche suggests, is to search with a purpose when seeking out new information. She points out, "We often default to surfing the internet out of habit rather than for an actual purpose, and wind up falling down the rabbit hole, reading article after article that doesn't really address any specific need for information. If you're going to research, do it with intention, and set a time limit."[63]

> "If you're going to research, do it with intention."[63]
>
> —Renee Goyeneche, marketing expert

Temporary Storage of Important Information

Business efficiency expert Lynne Cazaly frequently offers clients and the general public advice on how to resist or manage information overload. Of the many individual techniques she recommends, one is to utilize existing digital technology to help temporarily store data that will be important to access eventually but does not immediately need to be evaluated. She points out:

> Organizations often have digital knowledge management systems to store and retrieve important information. You can do the same to reduce brain clutter.
>
> I recommend creating a Word or Google document in which you write down information that your brain doesn't need to remember or store. In the early days of a new job, this is a clever way to offload the overload.
>
> For instance, a colleague, upon being hired, began her own type of Wikipedia page for the people, roles, products, and insights she needed to know in her new role. She reviewed the document every few days, adding information, emptying her brain and deliberately externalizing information into this self-made knowledge system.

Lynne Cazaly, "How to Save Yourself from 'Information Overload,'" *Harvard Business Review*, September 20, 2021. https://hbr.org.

Learning to Better Evaluate Information

Prioritizing tasks and trying to be more purposeful when searching for information have an added benefit. Namely, they make whatever data is taken in more reliable and useful. These are not the only ways that someone can learn to manage information intake, however. No less important a tool for achieving that goal is learning to be a better evaluator, or judge, of the quality of information. People can train themselves to view all new data critically. That is, individuals should test the information by applying a few simple, logical criteria, or standards.

One of those criteria is the currency, or timeliness, of the data. Was it released to the public recently or many years ago? As a rule of thumb, the more recent a batch of information is, the more likely it is to be up-to-date and accurate. Still, the currency of any data does depend on its nature. According to an authoritative website run by the Pennsylvania State University librarians, "While it is important that your information is current, keep in mind that 'recent' means different things in different disciplines. Ten years can be a good cutoff date, but it is important to realize that while in computer science ten years is completely outdated, in literary criticism ten years can be quite fresh."[64]

Another criterion applicable to new information is its relevance, or its importance to a person's needs. First, the person should decide whether the data relates to an ongoing project or answers a crucial question. If the data in question is not relevant and does not excite any interest, it should be ignored. If the information is relevant, the person should next determine whether it is at the appropriate reading level. If it is so technical and advanced that it requires a higher knowledge of the subject, or alternatively, if it is too simplistic and just repeats basic facts already known, it can and probably should be ignored.

One way to be more purposeful about looking for information is to evaluate its timeliness. In general, more current information is more likely to be accurate.

Tips on Quitting Social Media

Some of the people who say they are overwhelmed by information overload and want to learn to manage their information intake make the decision to quit using social media. This is partly because Facebook, Twitter, and other social media platforms are major contributors to the information glut. Also, frequent use of social media is a kind of addiction, and for some individuals that in itself is enough of a reason to quit. For anyone who might be contemplating doing that, information technology systems administrator Nicole Rennolds offers this advice:

Try uninstalling your social media apps for 12 hours at a time, and see if you can gradually increase the amount of time you go without using them. You can uninstall the apps without deactivating your accounts, which should help alleviate some of your anxiety. . . . Part of the reason why it's so hard to stay off social media is because of push notifications constantly interrupting us and reminding us to check our feed. If you're worried that turning off notifications entirely will cause you to miss important information, try using email notifications instead and just check them once or twice a day.

Nicole Rennolds, "How to Quit Social Media for Good," Makeuseof.com, January 11, 2021. www.makeuseof.com.

Still another standard of quality a person should use to judge new information is accuracy. In attempting to determine whether certain information is accurate, one should first determine whether it is backed up by evidence. If the author simply states something as fact but offers no evidence, it might not be accurate. If some evidence is provided, the reader should try to verify the data's accuracy by looking at other sources. Finally, the reader or viewer should check whether the author backs up claims by citing references, especially ones that seem reputable. "People make things up a lot more than we'd like," the Pennsylvania State librarians point out. "Citations or refer-

> "People make things up a lot more than we'd like. Citations or references to other research helps sift out what is authoritative from what is wishful thinking (or outright lies)."[65]
>
> —Pennsylvania State University librarians

ences to other research helps sift out what is authoritative from what is wishful thinking (or outright lies). What's more, if a useful article cites other useful articles, it makes it that much easier to find them."[65]

Rely on Respected Experts

Gauging the reliability of an author is perhaps the single most important task for someone trying to become a more skilled evaluator of information. Clearly, some human sources of information are more reliable than others; therefore, it is best to consult widely known and respected experts in their field. Moreover, it is always preferable to consult multiple experts on a subject to get varying but informed perspectives. In the words of the IvyPanda editors, "Looking for information is overwhelming. With so many voices, channels, and experts, it is hard to decide whom to trust. That's why it can lead to information overload, especially as some information can be overly redundant and repetitive. It would be easier to identify several experts whose opinion is valid and trustworthy."[66]

The New York Times *headquarters in New York City is pictured. One way to sort through an overwhelming amount of information is to look for information that comes from reputable sources, such as the* New York Times.

The experts in question can vary. They can be individual scholars, scientists, journalists, and so forth. They can also be collective sources such as certain reputable newspapers, journals, publishers, or online websites. There are no hard and fast rules for separating the reputable sources from the less reputable ones. But the Pennsylvania State librarians offer the following general rule of thumb:

> Newspapers like the *New York Times* and *Washington Post* are highly reputable, while news sources like the *Daily Beast* or the *Huffington Post* are of wildly variable quality [meaning they are only sometimes reliable]. Books from Oxford University Press and other university presses are of higher academic merit than [reputable yet less scholarly publishers such as] Random House. An encyclopedia article found on Wikipedia is more likely to be inaccurate than one found in the Gale Virtual Reference Library. A blog from the Chronicle of Higher Education is likely to be more reliable than a personal Word Press blog, and so on.[67]

There is no magic spell that can turn a person who feels inundated by the ongoing flood of information into a carefree, accomplished evaluator of data. Individuals must learn that skill a little at a time. In the meantime, however, anyone can begin to alleviate the pressure of information glut by following some advice offered by Renee Goyeneche: "If you're feeling overwhelmed, step back. Just because you *can* spend endless hours researching the state of the world and ruminating on what you discover, doesn't mean you *should*. Embrace the idea of 'all things in moderation.' You'll avoid information overload, and be happier and healthier for it."[68]

SOURCE NOTES

Introduction: Sifting Through the Noise

1. John Dean, "A Personal Experience with Information Anxiety/Overload," Verdict, February 20, 2015. https://verdict.justia.com.
2. Dean, "A Personal Experience with Information Anxiety/Overload."
3. Quoted in Laura Shin, "10 Steps to Conquering Information Overload," *Forbes*, November 14, 2014. www.forbes.com.
4. Quoted in Shin, "10 Steps to Conquering Information Overload."
5. Peter Landau, "Save Yourself! 7 Ways to Avoid Information Overload," ProjectManager, July 3, 2019. www.projectmanager.com.

Chapter One: The Causes and Effects of Information Overload

6. Stephen Altrogge, "How to Stop Information Overload from Crushing You," *Freedom* (blog), June 19, 2021. https://freedom.to/blog.
7. Altrogge, "How to Stop Information Overload from Crushing You."
8. Altrogge, "How to Stop Information Overload from Crushing You."
9. Alvin Toffler, *Future Shock*. New York: Bantam, 1970, p. 157.
10. Hitesh Bhasin, "Information Overload: Definition, Causes, and How to Avoid It," Marketing91, 2019. www.marketing91.com.
11. John B. Horrigan, "Worries About Information Overload Are Not Widespread," Pew Research Center, December 7, 2016. www.pewresearch.org.
12. Jutimoni Kalita, "Information Overload: Let's Understand and Tackle It," Story Mug, June 17, 2021. https://thestorymug.com.
13. Sean Illing, "Why You (Probably) Won't Finish Reading This Story," *Conversations* (podcast), Vox, February 8, 2022. www.vox.com.
14. Illing, "Why You (Probably) Won't Finish Reading This Story."
15. Quoted in Illing, "Why You (Probably) Won't Finish Reading This Story."
16. Quoted in Illing, "Why You (Probably) Won't Finish Reading This Story."

17. Quoted in Illing, "Why You (Probably) Won't Finish Reading This Story."
18. insideBIGDATA Editorial Team, "Overwhelmed by Data? Here's How to Get Control of It," insideBIGDATA, December 24, 2018. https://insidebigdata.com.
19. insideBIGDATA Editorial Team, "Overwhelmed by Data?"
20. Jill Huettich, "The Ultimate Guide to Managing Information Overload," MindManager, February 10, 2020. https://blog.mindmanager.com.

Chapter Two: How Information Overload Affects the Brain

21. Lawrence Taylor, personal interview with the author, February 27, 2022.
22. Taylor, interview.
23. Taylor, interview.
24. Landau, "Save Yourself!"
25. Srini Pillay, "The Ways Your Brain Manages Overload, and How to Improve Them," *Harvard Business Review*, June 7, 2017. https://hbr.org.
26. Pillay, "The Ways Your Brain Manages Overload, and How to Improve Them."
27. Pillay, "The Ways Your Brain Manages Overload, and How to Improve Them."
28. Kaori Ikeda and Hayley Teasdale, "How Our Memory Develops," Australian Academy of Science, 2022. www.science.org.au.
29. Ikeda and Teasdale, "How Our Memory Develops."
30. Philip E. Stieg et al., "Information Overload," Weill Cornell Brain and Spine Center, April 3, 2020. https://weillcornellbrainandspine.org.
31. Solarina Ho, "Older Adults Process Too Much Information, Leading to Cluttered Memories: Study," CTV News, February 14, 2022. https://www.ctvnews.ca.
32. Stieg et al, "Information Overload."
33. Jory MacKay, "Information Overload: Why We're Facing It and How to Handle It," *RescueTime* (blog), October 2, 2018. https://blog.rescuetime.com.

Chapter Three: Separating Information from Misinformation

34. Filippo Menczer and Thomas Hills, "Information Overload Helps Fake News Spread, and Social Media Knows It," *Scientific American*, December 1, 2020. www.scientificamerican.com.

35. Bhasin, "Information Overload."
36. David Dunning, "Gullible to Ourselves," in *The Social Psychology of Gullibility: Fake News, Conspiracy Theories, and Irrational Beliefs*, ed. Joseph P. Forgas and Roy F. Baumeister. London: Routledge, 2019, p. 217.
37. Dunning, "Gullible to Ourselves," p. 218.
38. Mike Loukides, "The Biggest Problem with Social Media Has Nothing to Do with Free Speech," Quartz, September 24, 2019. https://qz.com.
39. Quoted in Barbara Ortutay and David Klepper, "Virus Outbreak Means (Mis)information Overload: How to Cope," AP News, March 22, 2020. https://apnews.com.
40. Quoted in American Psychological Association, "Speaking of Psychology: Why People Believe in Conspiracy Theories, with Karen Douglas, PhD," 2021. www.apa.org.
41. Menczer and Hills, "Information Overload Helps Fake News Spread, and Social Media Knows It."

Chapter Four: Effects of Information Overload on Teens

42. Kevin Diaz, "We Are Running on Information Overload," *North Texas Daily*, March 25, 2021. www.ntdaily.com.
43. Diaz, "We Are Running on Information Overload."
44. Diaz, "We Are Running on Information Overload."
45. SchoolCNXT, "Information Overload from Too Many School Communications Sources," July 10, 2021. www.schoolcnxt.com.
46. SchoolCNXT, "Information Overload from Too Many School Communications Sources."
47. Quoted in Rachel Neha Shaw, "Information Overload: How Much Is Too Much?," Mustang Monthly, April 10, 2020. https://khsmustangmonthly.com.
48. Quoted in Shaw, "Information Overload."
49. Quoted in Lesley Lanir, "Digital Information Overload Overwhelms and Distracts Students," Medium, July 2, 2019. https://medium.com.
50. Quoted in Lanir, "Digital Information Overload Overwhelms and Distracts Students."
51. Quoted in Shaw, "Information Overload."
52. Quoted in Shaw, "Information Overload."
53. Quoted in Lanir, "Digital Information Overload Overwhelms and Distracts Students."

54. Kelly Bielefeld, "Information Overload Part Two: How Parents and Teachers Can Help Students," *Mimio Educator* (blog), February 27, 2018. https://blog.mimio.com.

Chapter Five: Learning to Avoid Information Overload

55. Chris, "How I Overcame Information Overload to Thrive on Less," *The Unconventional Route* (blog), January 30, 2022. www.theunconventionalroute.com.
56. Chris, "How I Overcame Information Overload to Thrive on Less."
57. Chris, "How I Overcame Information Overload to Thrive on Less."
58. Chris, "How I Overcame Information Overload to Thrive on Less."
59. Chris, "How I Overcame Information Overload to Thrive on Less."
60. Landau, "Save Yourself!"
61. IvyPanda, "How to Overcome Information Overload: Complete Guide 101," October 3, 2021. https://ivypanda.com.
62. IvyPanda, "How to Overcome Information Overload."
63. Renee Goyeneche, "How to Stop Information Overload in Its Tracks," *Forbes*, July 23, 2020. www.forbes.com.
64. Penn State University Libraries, "Evaluating Information," 2022. https://libraries.psu.edu.
65. Penn State University Libraries, "Evaluating Information."
66. IvyPanda, "How to Overcome Information Overload."
67. Penn State University Libraries, "Evaluating Information."
68. Goyeneche, "How to Stop Information Overload in Its Tracks."

FOR FURTHER RESEARCH

Books

Lynne Cazaly, *Argh! Too Much Information, Not Enough Brain: A Practical Guide to Outsmarting Overwhelm*. Melbourne, Australia: Cazaly Communications, 2021.

Rachel Ignotofsky, *The History of the Computer: People, Inventions, and Technology That Changed Our World*. Berkeley, CA: Ten-Speed, 2022.

Tamra B. Orr, *The Information Revolution*. New York: Lucent, 2019.

Cass R. Sunstein, *Too Much Information: Understanding What You Don't Want to Know*. Cambridge, MA: MIT Press, 2022.

Internet Sources

Stephen Altrogge, "How to Stop Information Overload from Crushing You," *Freedom* (blog), June 19, 2021. https://freedom.to/blog.

Solarina Ho, "Older Adults Process Too Much Information, Leading to Cluttered Memories: Study," CTV News, February 14, 2022. https://www.ctvnews.ca.

Sean Illing, "Why You (Probably) Won't Finish Reading This Story," *Conversations* (podcast), Vox, February 8, 2022. www.vox.com.

Indeed Editorial Team, "Information Overload: What It Is and 10 Tips for Avoiding It," Indeed, September 16, 2021. www.indeed.com.

Christian Jarrett, "A Psychologist Explains Why People Believe in Conspiracy Theories," Science Focus, January 5, 2022. www.sciencefocus.com.

Georgien Modijefsky, "The Dangers of Information Overload and How to Prevent It," Workspace 365, September 8, 2021. https://workspace365.net.

National Today, "Information Overload Day—October 20, 2022," October 20, 2022. https://nationaltoday.com.

Louise Perry, "In a World of Information Overload, the Challenge Is to Avoid Being Driven Mad," *New Statesman*, September 29, 2021. www.newstatesman.com.

Trish Sammer, "What a 13th-Century Monk Can Teach Us About Managing Information Overload," *Work Life* (blog), Atlassian, February 19, 2021. www.atlassian.com.

Seed Scientific, "How Much Data Is Created Every Day?," October 28, 2021. https://seedscientific.com.

Websites

Digital Wellbeing
https://wellbeing.google
This useful site suggests ways that people can feel less distracted by the flood of information generated by modern technology and use that technology to better achieve their personal goals.

Information Overload Research Group
https://iorgforum.org
This valuable source provides links to various sites that discuss information overload and how to keep from being overwhelmed by it.

National Association for Media Literacy Education (NAMLE)
https://namle.net
NAMLE is devoted to helping individuals and the public in general to achieve media literacy, as well as to avoid misinformation and cope with information overload.

News Literacy Project
https://newslit.org
The nonprofit News Literary Project presents various resources for both educators and the public that show how people can avoid misinformation and become smart, active consumers of news and other information.

Teens for Press Freedom (TPF)
www.teensforpressfreedom.org
TPF is a national organization run by young people whose mission is to promote freedom of the press and to help students learn to separate fact from fiction in news reports.

INDEX

Note: Boldface page numbers indicate illustrations.

Altrogge, Stephen, 8–9, 10
attention span, decreased, 12–14
    impact on workplace productivity, 15–17

Bhasin, Hitesh, 10, 29–30
Bielefeld, Kelly, 47
brain, 5
    data accumulation and, 7
    impact of information overload on, 19–20, 24–25
    multitasking and, 27
    transformation of information into memory and, 20–23
Bukacek, Annie, 32

Cazaly, Lynne, 52
Centers for Disease Control and Prevention, 32
Chronicle of Higher Education, 56
Clinton, Hillary, 33, 34, **34**
confirmation bias, 36–37
conspiracy theories, 34–37
COVID-19 pandemic, 26
    deadly disinformation about, 32
    false theories about, 35–36

Daily Beast (blog), 56
Dean, John, 4
Diaz, Kevin, 38–39
Digital Wellbeing (website), 62
Douglas, Karen, 35, 37
Dunning, David, 30, 31

Facebook, 5, 20, 31, 39
    use by Russian hackers, 33
Fauci, Anthony, 36
feedback loops, 31–33
Future Shock (Toffler), 5, 9

Gale Virtual Reference Library, 56
Google, 47
Goyeneche, Renee, 51, 56
Gross, Bertram Myron, 5

Hari, Johann, 13–14
Hilliard, Robert, 12
Hills, Thomas, 29, 37
Ho, Solarina, 25
Horrigan, John B., 10
Huettich, Jill, 17
Huffington Post (blog), 56

Ikeda, Kaori, 21, 23
Illing, Sean, 12, 13
information
    amount available, 9
    distinguishing needed from unneeded, 49–51
    gauging reliability of sources of, 55–56
    important, temporary storage of, 52
    methods of evaluating, 52–55
    sources of, before internet, 30
    transformation into memory, 20–23
information overload, 4–5
    causes of, 10
    conspiracy theories enhanced by, 35
    decreased use of traditional information sources and, 46–47
    distorted sense of time and, 44–46
    impact on students, 38–39, 41–42
    social media as major contributor to, 54
Information Overload Research Group, 62
insideBIGDATA (online technology site), 16, 17
internet
    average amount of time per day spent on, 12

distracted behaviors and, 44
information sources prior to, 30
limiting students' use of, 46
as source of information glut, 5
IvyPanda (website), 50–51, 55

Justman, Jessica, 35

Kalita, Jutimoni, 11

Landau, Peter, 7, 19, 50
Levitin, Daniel, 5–6, 7
Loukides, Mike, 33
Lynas, Mark, 32

MacKay, Jory, 27
Madore, Kevin P., 22
Marketing91 (website), 10
memory, transformation of information into, 20–23
Menczer, Filippo, 29, 37
multitasking, 9
information glut and urge to, 25–27
as inefficient/counterproductive, 22
stress and, 27

National Association for Media Literacy Education (NAMLE), 62
News Literacy Project, 62
New York Times (newspaper), **55**, 56

older adults, information overload in, 24–25
opinion polls. *See* surveys
Oxford University Press, 56

Pennsylvania State University, 53, 54–55, 56
Pew Research Center, 43
Pillay, Srini, 19, 26
polls. *See* surveys
presidential election, 2016, 33

Rainie, Lee, 44, 46–47
Random House, 56
Rennolds, Nicole, 54
Rolling Stone (magazine), 32
Rotman Research Institute, 25

SchoolCNXT, 40, 41, 46
school information sources, 39–41
Shaw, Rachel Neha, 41, 42, 44–45
social media
tips on quitting, 54
use for research, 47
Soleimani, Qasem, 45, **45**
Stieg, Philip E., 24, 25–26, 27
Stolen Focus (Hari), 13
stress
from information glut, 11
multitasking and, 27
surveys
on resources used for research, 47
of teachers on impact of digital technology, 44

Taylor, Lawrence, 18–19
Teasdale, Hayley, 21, 23
Teens for Press Freedom (TPF), 62
Toffler, Alvin, 5, 9
Trump, Donald, 33
Twitter, 12, 39, 54

Wagner, Anthony D., 22
Wallace, David Foster, 5
Washington Post (newspaper), 56
Wikipedia, 52, 56
percentage of student using for research, 47
World Health Organization (WHO), 12–13

YouTube, 9
COVID disinformation on, 32
number of videos viewed daily on, 12
use for research, 47